The
Gigantic
Turnip

For Owen — N.S.

Barefoot Beginners
an imprint of
Barefoot Books
PO Box 95
Kingswood
Bristol BS30 5BH

Hardback ISBN 1 902283 11 2
Paperback ISBN 1 902283 29 5

Graphic design by Tom Grzelinski, England
Colour reproduction by Grafiscan, Verona
Printed in Singapore by Tien Wah Press Pte Ltd

3 5 7 9 8 6 4

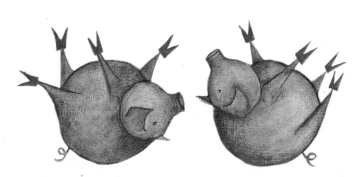

The Gigantic Turnip

Aleksei Tolstoy
&
Niamh Sharkey

BAREFOOT BOOKS
BATH

Long
ago, an
old man
and an
old woman
lived together
in a crooked
old cottage
with a large,
overgrown
garden.

The old man
and the old
woman

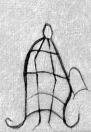

kept six yellow canaries,

five white geese,

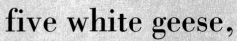

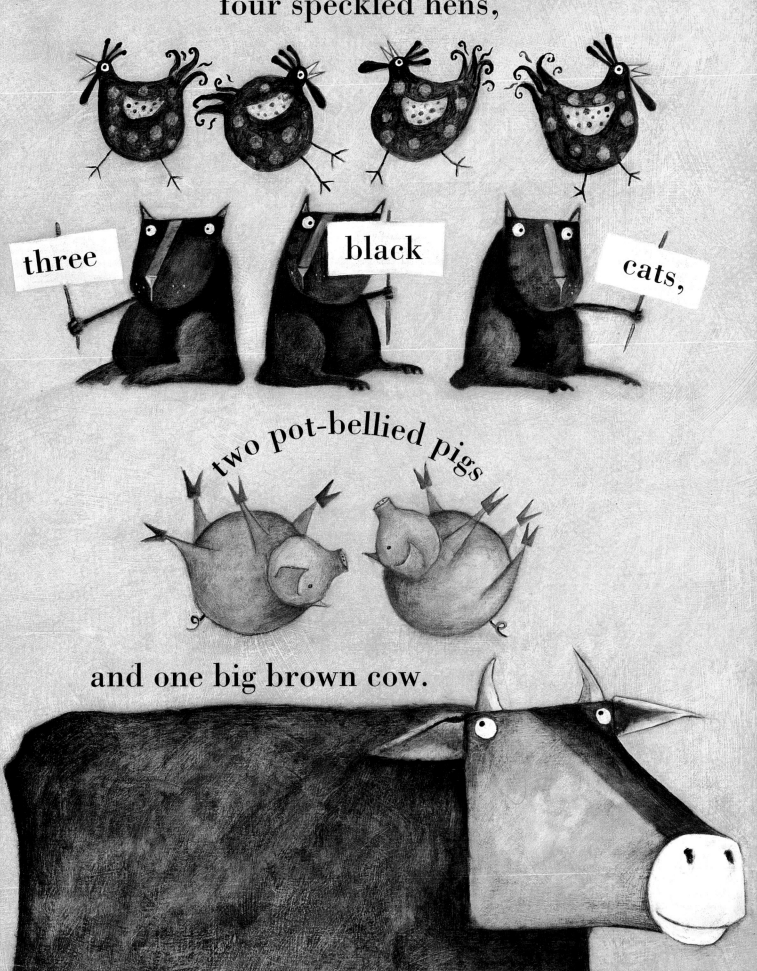

On a fine March morning, the old woman sat up in bed, sniffed the sweet spring air and said, 'It's time for us to sow the vegetables!' So the old man and the old woman went out into the garden.

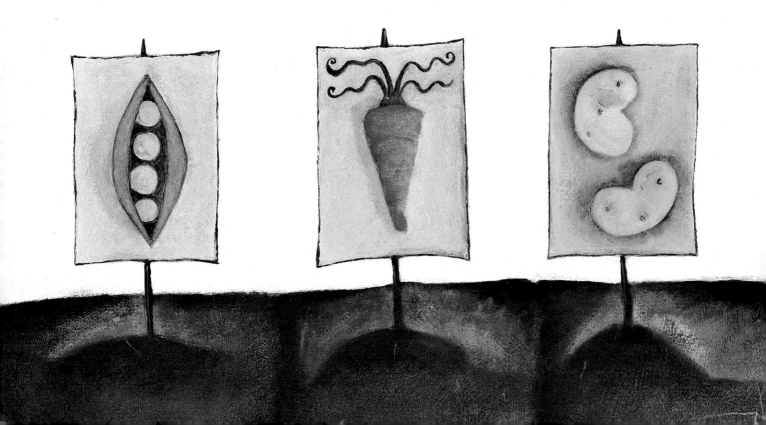

They sowed peas and carrots
and potatoes and beans. Last of
all, they sowed
turnips.

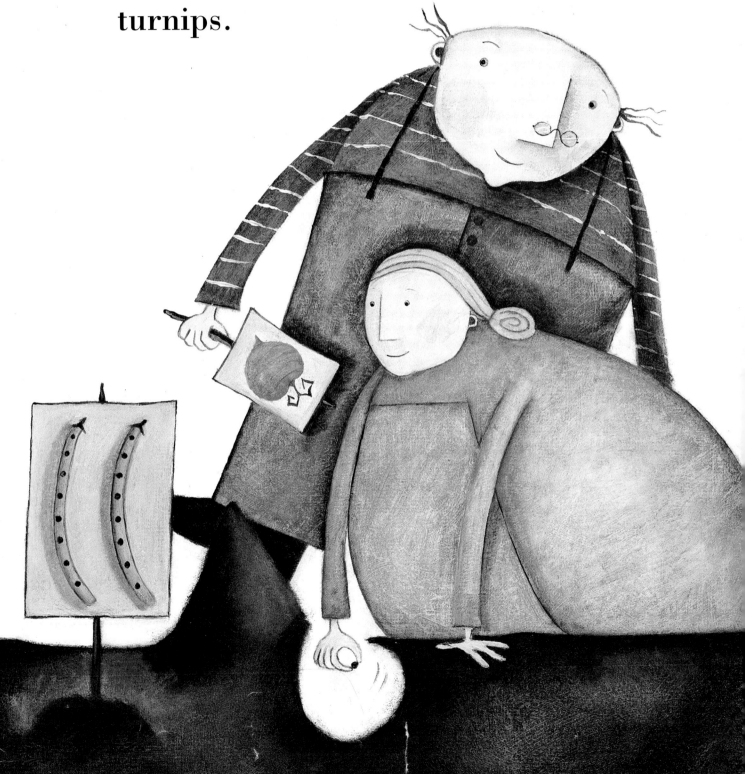

That night, rain fell — pitter, patter! — on the garden of the crooked old cottage. The old man and the old woman smiled as they slept.

The rain would help the seeds swell and produce fine juicy vegetables.

Spring passed and the summer sun ripened the vegetables. The old man and the old woman harvested their carrots and potatoes and peas and beans and turnips. At the end of the row, there was just one turnip left. It looked very big.
In fact, it looked

gigantic.

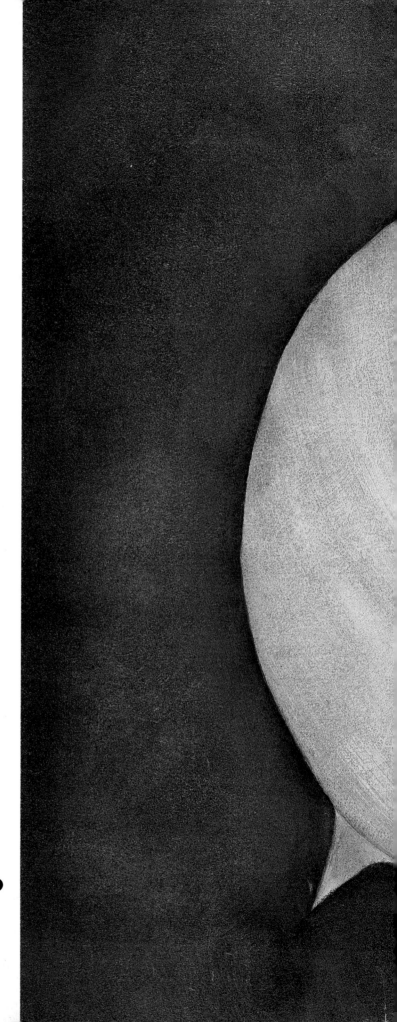

On a fine
September
morning, the
old man sat up
in bed, sniffed
the cool autumn
air and said,
'It's time for us to
pull up that turnip.'

And out he went.

The old man pulled and
heaved and tugged and
yanked, but the turnip
would not move.

The old man went to find
the old woman.

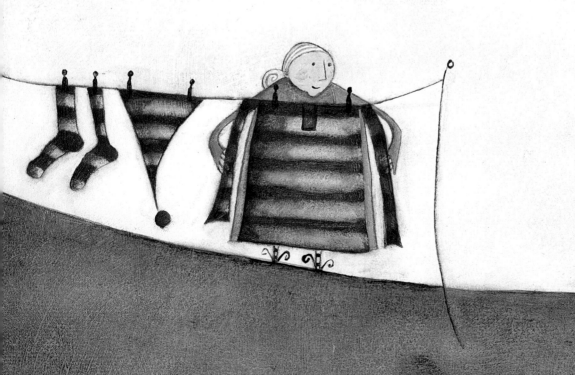

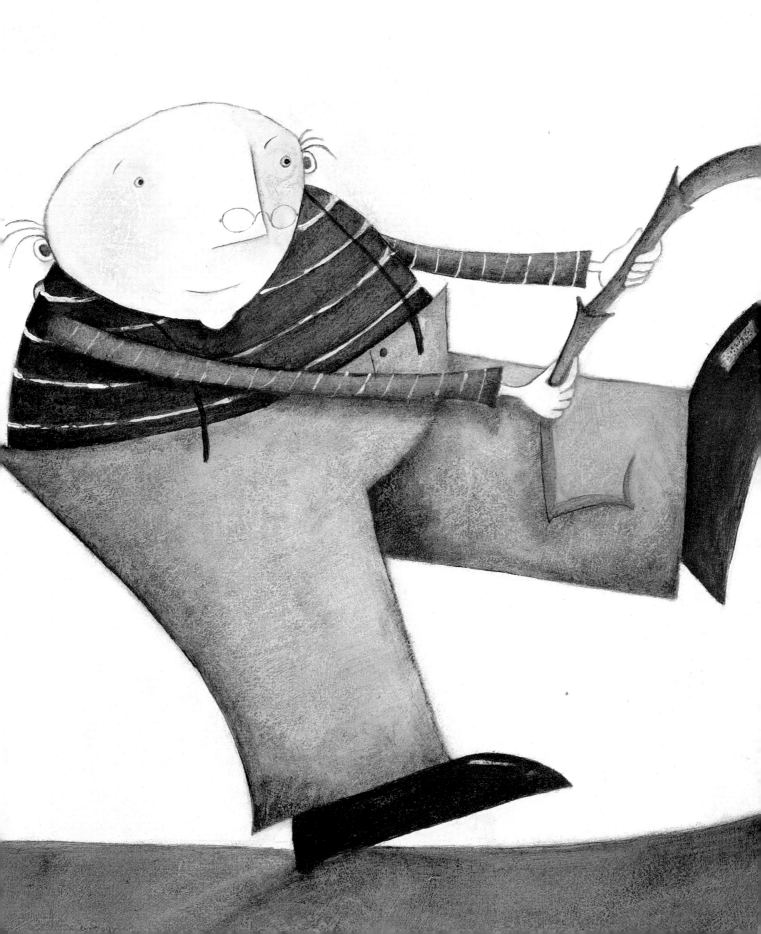

The old woman wrapped her arms round the old man's waist. Both of them pulled and heaved and tugged and yanked, but still the turnip would not move.

So the old woman went to fetch the big brown cow.

The old man, the old woman and the big brown cow pulled and heaved and tugged and yanked, but still the turnip would not move.

So the old man mopped his brow and went to fetch the two pot-bellied pigs.

The old man, the old woman,
the big brown cow and the two
pot-bellied pigs pulled and
heaved and tugged and yanked.
Still the turnip would not move.

So the old woman rolled up her
sleeves and went to fetch the
three black cats.

The old man, the old
woman, the big brown
cow, the two pot-bellied
pigs and the three black
cats pulled and heaved
and tugged and yanked.
Still the turnip would
not move.

So one of the cats
twitched her tail and
went to fetch the four
speckled hens.

The old man, the old
woman, the big brown
cow, the two pot-bellied
pigs, the three black cats
and the four speckled
hens pulled and heaved
and tugged and yanked.
Still the turnip would
not move.

So one of the hens shook
her feathers and went to
fetch the five white geese.

The old man, the old woman, the big brown cow, the two pot-bellied pigs, the three black cats, the four speckled hens and the five white geese pulled and heaved and tugged and yanked. Still the turnip would not move.

So one of the geese
craned her neck and
went to fetch the
six yellow canaries.

The old man, the old woman, the big brown cow, the two pot-bellied pigs, the three black cats, the four speckled hens,

the five white geese and the
six yellow canaries pulled
and heaved and tugged
and yanked.

Still the turnip would not move.

The old man scratched his head.

The animals and birds lay
on the ground gasping.

The old woman had an idea.

The old woman went
into the kitchen and
put a piece of cheese
by the mousehole.
Soon a hungry little
mouse popped its
head out of the hole.
The old woman
caught the mouse and
carried it outside.

The old man, the old woman, the big brown cow, the two pot-bellied pigs, the three black cats, the four speckled hens,

the five white geese, the
six yellow canaries and the
hungry little mouse pulled
and heaved and tugged
and yanked.

Pop!

The gigantic turnip came flying out of the ground and everyone fell over. The canaries fell on the mouse, the geese fell on the canaries, the hens fell on the geese, the cats fell on the hens, the pigs fell on the cats, the cow fell on the pigs, the old woman fell on the cow and the old man fell on the old woman.

All of them lay on the ground and laughed.

That night the old man and
the old woman made a huge
bowl of turnip stew.
Everyone ate as much as
they could. And do you know
what? The hungry little
mouse ate the most of all.

and they hugged their very own

Hugh Shampoo!